D1239159

Mary J. Blige

Diane Bailey

ROSEN
PUBLISHING

New York

Published in 2009 by The Rosen Publishing Group, Inc.
29 East 21st Street, New York, NY 10010

First Edition

Library of Congress Cataloging-in-Publication Data

Bailey, Diane, 1966–
Mary J. Blige / Diane Bailey.—1st ed.
    p. cm.—(The library of hip-hop biographies)
Includes bibliographical references, discography, and index.
ISBN-13: 978-1-4358-5055-2 (library binding)
ISBN-13: 978-1-4358-5441-3 (pbk)
ISBN-13: 978-1-4358-5447-5 (6 pack)
1. Blige, Mary J.—Juvenile literature. 2. Rap musicians—United
States—Biography—Juvenile literature. I. Title.
ML3930.B585B35 2009
782.421643092—dc22
[B]
                                                    2008012607

Manufactured in the United States of America

On the cover: Mary J. Blige performs at the Pepsi Smash Super Bowl
XLII Bash in 2008.

CONTENTS

INTRODUCTION

There's a certain something about Mary J. Blige. But what exactly is it? Well, for one thing, the woman can sing. Her voice has the smoky soul of the great rhythm and blues (R & B) singers, and she wraps it around the edgy beats of the hip-hop culture in which she grew up.

But there's more. There's something that goes beyond the quality of her voice or the melodies in her songs or the catchiness of her beats. There's something in her music that can't be tinkered with by a soundman with a mixing board. It's the same quality that she had when she first started: honesty. It was probably that—more than anything else—that earned her the title "Queen of Hip-Hop Soul."

In the 1990s, hip-hop soul emerged as a subgenre of R & B. It's rougher than traditional R & B, and it has a lot of rap influences. It's also a genre in which artists tackle the hard parts of life, like poverty, abuse, and racism. It was the perfect outlet for Blige. She made a name for herself by singing about the troubles she went through growing up in a rough, urban neighborhood. The pain in her life showed through in her music. Later, when her life improved, her joy came through, too. But either way, it was honest. Blige won her fans by singing what she knew to be true.

She's a rags-to-riches story for African American girls. Her career has lasted twenty years—so far—and there's no sign of it slowing down. Her music has sold forty million records. She's won scores of major music awards. Her fans regularly vote her as their favorite performer.

But behind the bodyguards, underneath the piles of awards, inside the glamorous exterior, Mary J. Blige is the same person she started as: an around-the-way girl from New York.

CHAPTER ONE
FINDING A VOICE

The sounds coming out of Mary Jane Blige's apartment in New York City were of music. Born on January 11, 1971, she grew up listening to soul music. Her mother, Cora, played the songs of Otis Redding and Al Green. She played the songs of Gladys Knight and Aretha Franklin. One of Blige's earliest memories is of hearing Roy Ayers's "Everybody Loves the Sunshine," a song that moves her to this day.

Gladys Knight and the Pips, shown here in 1978, was a group that had an early influence on Mary J. Blige.

Blige and her older sister, LaTonya, listened. And they sang. They were always singing. Mary sang in front of the mirror, a hairbrush doubling as her microphone. She remembers going to the Hudson River and singing. She wanted to hear how her voice sounded across the water. Her mother remembers her singing along to *Sesame Street*—and doing it well. "She was three years old when I recognized her gift," Cora said in a 2001 interview with *Rolling Stone* magazine. When Blige was seven years old, she won a talent show for her singing. And that was just the beginning.

7

BORN AT THE SAME TIME

Inside her apartment, Blige's mother played soul music. But outside the doors, a new kind of music was taking over. Like Blige herself, something else was born in New York City in the 1970s. It was hip-hop.

Hip-hop came from young people. It came from urban neighborhoods filled with African Americans and Latinos. Hip-hop had its own energetic style. It was a perfect fit for young people eager to get out of the house and move. You couldn't just put a hip-hop record on the turntable and sit back and listen. Hip-hop insisted that its listeners get up and join in.

It also needed a disc jockey (DJ) to get it going. First, the DJ would play the danceable beat in a song—the "break." Right before the break ended, he would switch to another turntable with the same record on it. It was all cued up to play the break again. He would switch back and forth, playing the funky beat over and over. "Scratching"— moving the needle of a vinyl record back and forth on the groove—produced a distinctive sound that became a hip-hop trademark.

The sound spread through the streets as DJs used the electricity from streetlights to power their speakers. Sometimes, DJs decided to talk over the words, often in rhyme. This was the beginning of modern rap.

At first, some people weren't sure that hip-hop should even be called music. After all, the most important part of the music didn't even have notes. Instead, the beat was king. The most important musician wasn't playing an instrument; he was spinning a turntable and holding a microphone.

Whether or not hip-hop was actual "music," it did go beyond the musical world. It was a whole cultural movement that also included break dancing and graffiti. Through music, movement, and art, an entire generation of young people found a way to express themselves.

Break dancing was the ultimate street entertainment for New Yorkers in the early 1980s.

In a way, hip-hop was like a member of Mary J. Blige's family. The first record she ever bought was "Rapper's Delight" by the Sugarhill Gang, which came out in 1979. "Rapper's Delight" wasn't the first rap song, but it was the first one to make it big.

In a 2006 interview with BallerStatus.com, she said, "Hip-hop is the foundation of Mary J. Blige. Hip-hop is the reason why my music even exists . . . I never let it die. It's a part of Mary J. Blige."

A SAFE HAVEN

There was one place that Mary J. Blige felt safe: church. Nobody hurt her in church. Nobody made her feel bad. Plus, she could sing. People loved listening to her. She was one of a lot of African American singers who got their start by singing in church. Even as a child, Blige was putting her own spin on things. In an interview with Yahoo! Music in 2003, she recalled that the congregation tended to sing sad songs. She didn't want to sing sad songs! She would go home, punch up the rhythm, and return to sing new upbeat versions.

Blige made the music her own, but she was also careful not to make it too different. Even back then, she knew that she wanted to touch her audience—and her audience was mostly the older people at church. "We never tried to take it out of the element," she said. "We tried to put it in the middle, so everybody would be happy."

BECOMING HER ENVIRONMENT

Hip-hop stuck with Blige, but unfortunately, so did other parts of her environment. When she was four, her parents split up. Cora, LaTonya, and Mary moved to Savannah, Georgia, where Blige's grandmother lived.

After about a year, however, the family moved back to New York. They settled in Yonkers, New York, where they lived in a government housing project. The "projects" were meant to provide affordable housing for people who didn't have much money. Many of the projects, including the one where Blige lived, also had a lot of problems. She was surrounded by people who drank alcohol and did drugs. She saw women being hit.

Cora, a nurse, was a working single mother, and sometimes babysitters took care of the girls. Blige revealed years later that one male caretaker assaulted her.

By the time Blige moved out of the projects, she had seen a lot of violence. She had a scar, just under her left eye, which she now refuses to talk about. But the deeper wounds were emotional ones. All her life, she had lived around people who didn't want her to become anything. Unfortunately, she says, those people even included her own family.

Blige's father, Thomas, had been in and out—mostly out—of her life. He was a jazz musician, though, and she remembers that he was the one who taught her to harmonize—a skill that would serve her for the rest of her life.

Mostly, though, she remembers that her family did not encourage her singing. Cora had wanted to be a singer, and Blige has said that jealousy may have stopped her mother from helping her to fulfill her dream.

By the time Blige was sixteen years old, she felt beaten down by her environment. Everyone around her seemed to be doing drugs and drinking alcohol, and she had started to do those things as well. When she was a junior in high school, she dropped out—a move she later called a mistake. She had a few odd jobs such as working as a cashier at a department store. Sometimes, she styled hair for her friends and neighbors. But mostly, Blige was drifting around with no clear purpose. "I ended up becoming my environment," she said in a 2007 interview with *Parade* magazine. "It was bigger than me."

A DAY AT THE MALL

One day, Blige and her friends went to a shopping mall in nearby White Plains, New York. There was a place at the mall where people could record themselves singing. Blige sang Anita Baker's hit "Caught Up in the Rapture." She loved the tape that she made. Her mother's boyfriend thought it was good, too. One day, he asked to borrow it. He knew some people who worked in the music industry and he wanted them to listen to it. Who knew what might happen?

The people he knew were not in a position to launch Blige's career. But the tape made its way into different hands. Friends passed it along to friends, and finally it came to Andre Harrell. Harrell was president of a small record company called Uptown Records. He liked the tape so much that he offered Blige a contract. And she signed it—in the laundry room of her apartment complex. She became Uptown's youngest artist, and its only girl!

Over the next few years, she would do session work, singing backup for the label's other artists. In 1990, she sang backup for

Jeff Redd in a live show at the Apollo Theater in Harlem, New York. Then came the song "I'll Do 4 U," by rap artist Father MC. Blige sang the "hook"— the line that is repeated throughout the song. She was also in the video. She was still in the background, but she was finally getting to do what she liked best—singing.

Producers Andre Harrell (left) and Sean "Diddy" Combs (right) gave Blige her start at Uptown Records.

At Uptown, Blige was surrounded by people who knew music. Soon, she would meet a man who would help shape her future career. He was an unknown, just like her. But he would also become a successful artist and producer. His name was Sean Combs. His nickname was Puff Daddy, and today he's known as Diddy. Blige called him Puffy.

At the time, Combs was just starting out at Uptown as an A & R executive. A & R stands for "artists and repertoire." A & R executives find new musical groups for a record label.

When Combs heard a tape of Blige singing, he heard talent. He heard potential. Put together, he heard a future star.

CHAPTER TWO

SHAPING A STYLE

Mary J. Blige was like a diamond in the rough. Yes, she had talent, but in the music business, it takes more than just a good voice to become a star. Stars need style. Sean "Diddy" Combs helped Blige to develop an image. He found edgy songs that matched her rough voice. She started wearing hip street clothes. The "Jane" in her name became a punchy "J." She took etiquette and speech classes. She was learning to be a star.

Thanks to Combs, Blige changed from an insecure eighteen-year-old into an up-and-coming star.

In this photo, Mary J. Blige, performing in 1992, dresses the part of a street-smart girl. The image helped her win fans when she was starting out.

SING IT LIKE IT IS

In 1992, when she was only twenty-one years old, Blige released her first album, *What's the 411?* She had once worked as a telephone operator, and the album begins with the sound of a ringing phone. The name was appropriate for another reason: Blige was going to tell her audience the "real deal."

What's the 411? was an instant success. It sold more than two million copies. A platinum album is one that has sold a million copies. So, with her debut album, Blige had gone multiplatinum!

Two songs from the album, "You Remind Me" and "Real Love," became crossover hits. "Crossover" means that a song in one genre becomes popular with listeners in other genres. Both songs were number one on the R & B charts and in the Top 40 on the pop charts.

The music industry took notice. Blige was nominated for several awards, and in 1993 she won two Soul Train Music Awards, including one for Best New Artist.

She found even more success with her next album, *My Life*, which came out in late 1994. Once again, she teamed up with Combs to produce it. However, she took a stronger hand in this album. Combs had encouraged her to write songs, and on this album, she participated in writing almost all of them.

What could be simpler than the title *My Life*? That's what it was—Blige laid out the circumstances of her life. She sang about her feelings. On this album, the sound had a little less of a rap feel, and it was a little darker. It marked the beginning of Blige's move into a deeper soul sound. The title track was a tribute to Roy Ayers's "Everybody Loves the Sunshine," a song she loved as a child. The song came out easily. She wrote it in only a few hours, but it had an enduring power. In it, Blige indeed sang about her life and the pain she had gone through— the pain she was still going through. With her honesty, she won her fans. She later said that the album was her way of asking for help.

In a 2005 interview with the UK's *Guardian* newspaper, she said, "I had no idea that my personal pain would create such a big fan base. Everything that was bringing me down was everything that rose me up."

THE 411 ON BLING

Think stiletto heels and rhinestone-studded T-shirts, faux-fur bags and gold chains. If it is expensive and designer, it's "bling." And no one wears the look of bling better than Mary J. Blige. Although the look is sometimes criticized as being overdone and tacky, Blige has given it her own spin—and she pulls it off.

When she was starting out, other artists wore super-sexy clothing and glamorous jewelry. But she found a different style. Some people say Blige created the "ghetto fabulous" look. Her glamorous outfits were equipped to walk the streets—literally. Combat boots were her trademark fashion statement. She brought everything down a notch, making her look fit the tough street neighborhoods she had grown up in. She wasn't forgetting her roots in either her music or her image.

"Other people have to go out, follow what's happening. I just do what I do, and people follow me," Blige told the UK's *Guardian* newspaper in 2005. Now, she watches old James Bond movies for fashion inspiration. And when she starts to see too many people who look like her, she changes her look.

GOING HER OWN WAY

Once again, several songs from *My Life* were crossover hits, and Blige was at the top of Billboard's R & B charts. The album debuted at number one on the R & B charts, and it eventually sold three million copies—another multiplatinum accomplishment.

She branched out with some other musical projects. She covered Aretha Franklin's "(You Make Me Feel Like) A Natural Woman" for the Fox TV show *New York Undercover*. She sang "Not Gon' Cry," a hit song from her third album, *Share My World*, for the film *Waiting to Exhale*. The movie's soundtrack also featured other famous singers such as Whitney Houston and Toni Braxton. Blige was playing with the big girls.

She also joined forces with Method Man, a rap artist, on a duet of "I'll Be There for You/You're All I Need to Get By." That song earned Blige her first Grammy Award, in 1996.

By now, Sean Combs was beginning to work with other artists—young, female artists, like Blige herself. She couldn't deal with that, so she broke off ties with him. She did her next album, 1997's *Share My World*, by herself.

This one had even more of a soul sound. Critics were divided on what they thought about it. Some liked it. Others were disappointed. They said Blige was losing some of her hip-hop appeal with a more traditional R & B sound. But her fans weren't disappointed. The album went triple platinum. She also won an American Music Award for Favorite Album in the Soul/R & B category.

Blige holds her own as she practices with other divas for the 1997 Grammy Awards program (from left: Brandy, Whitney Houston, CeCe Winans, and Blige).

She went on tour with *Share My World*, reaching out to the fans who had supported her and made her a star. The tour was so successful that she made another album using her live performances. That album, *The Tour*, was also a success.

In 1999, Blige was ready to release her fourth studio album. This one had the most straightforward, open title yet. It was simply called *Mary*. By now, she had developed her own unique style, but she had also learned from many artists along the way. This album paid tribute through a method called sampling."

Sampling is using parts of another song. For example, the single "Deep Inside" used parts of Elton John's hit "Bennie and the Jets."

Sampling is a hip-hop trademark, but the sound of *Mary* was more soul than hip-hop. Many critics liked *Mary*. Others thought she had failed in her effort to make herself seem more adult and mainstream. Maybe the bigger question was, "Would Mary lose her fans?"

The answer was no. Although the album didn't sell quite as well, it was far from a failure. Blige was changing, her music was changing, and her fans were right there along with her.

ALL THE WRONG PEOPLE

Although Blige was finding success with music, she wasn't having much luck in other areas of her life. With the money she was making, she bought clothes, shoes, and jewelry. But buying things didn't make her happy. Her boyfriend was K-Ci Hailey, a member of the popular R & B group Jodeci, but the relationship was rocky and not good for her.

People had told her that she would never be anyone, and she had proved them wrong. But now, the people surrounding Blige were still bringing her down. She felt that they didn't care about her. They only cared about what she could do for them. Drink and drugs still surrounded her, and she didn't have the confidence to turn away from these temptations herself.

Blige dated K-Ci Hailey *(left, pictured with brother JoJo Hailey)*, but the relationship didn't work out.

The problem had started in high school, and now it was getting worse. It interfered with her career.

She also got a reputation for being surly and difficult to please. Her quick temper got her into trouble. She was late for interviews and photo shoots. Sometimes, she didn't show up at all. One time, at a show in London, the audience booed her off the stage.

Blige struggled with the same problems that she'd had all her life. She didn't like herself. She thought she was ugly. She didn't think she was worth much. She was floundering. At one point, Blige told *Parade* in 2007, she thought about killing herself.

She knew she had to make some changes. Her very life was in danger, and the threat came from within herself. It came from the choices that she was making every day.

CHAPTER THREE

MAKING IT AS MARY

Something—many things, actually—had to change, and Mary J. Blige knew it. She was spiraling downward. She was beginning to understand that no one was going to change her except herself. That didn't mean that no one could help. She just had to get rid of the wrong people in her life and find the right ones. She took a hard look at her life and made some decisions. One of them was to become involved with a record producer named Kendu Isaacs.

THE LOVE OF HER LIFE

Blige met Isaacs in 2000. Fellow musician Queen Latifah wanted her to sing on a song for her album. Blige was on tour, but they juggled their schedules and arranged to meet one day at a studio in Detroit, Michigan. Latifah came with her producer, Isaacs. The three of them worked through the afternoon.

Blige remembers the spark that she felt upon meeting Isaacs. But she thought he and Latifah were

Music producer Kendu Isaacs is the man for Mary J. Blige. They met in 2000 and married in 2003.

a couple, so she didn't say anything. Later, she found out that they weren't together. She also found out that Isaacs had been attracted to her as well. With Latifah playing matchmaker, Blige and Isaacs finally got together several months later.

They clicked immediately, but it was more than just a boy-meets-girl attraction. He recognized that she had problems. In one of their first phone calls, Isaacs told her that he had to tell her some things that might hurt. Blige wasn't expecting that. She wasn't sure that she wanted to hear what he had to say.

But Isaacs explained that he sensed her pain. He wanted to help her work through it. The process would hurt, but in the end she would be better because of it. "Those words from Kendu woke my spirit up," she told *Essence* magazine in June 2007.

Also, Isaacs had a stable life. He was a Christian and had a loving family. "When I saw his life, that's the life I wanted," she told the *Guardian* in 2005.

Even after she met him, however, Blige still spent a lot of time partying. For a while, Isaacs put up with it. But one day, before a show, she overheard him say that if she came home drunk that day, he would leave her. The words struck Blige. That night, she came home sober.

That same night, they received a phone call.

THE SUMMER OF 2001

The United States was about to experience a horrific tragedy. It was only two weeks before 9/11. But the phone call that she and Isaacs received that night was about another plane crash— one that would change Blige's life.

This crash was an accident, not a terrorist act. On the plane, however, was someone that she knew. She was a young, black female singer named Aaliyah who was called the "Princess of Hip-Hop Soul." Blige didn't know Aaliyah well, but the accident affected her profoundly. "At the end of the day, I knew I was next," she told the *Guardian*. "I just thought, 'I'm scared.'"

Fans constructed a shrine *[above]* to the singer Aaliyah after she died in a plane crash in 2001—an accident that Blige says helped her change her own life.

She felt that people in the music business did not care about her welfare. If she were to die, they would not mourn the death of Mary J. Blige, the person. They would only be looking to replace Mary J. Blige, the moneymaking star.

She decided she needed to protect herself. She needed to take control of her career and her life. The first step was to stop messing up her body with drugs and alcohol. After all, she had just released an album called *No More Drama*. Perhaps she should start with herself. She also knew Isaacs would support her as she took those first difficult steps.

Barely two weeks later, the whole world was shaken by the events of 9/11. But during this horrible, stressful time, Blige says, she did not turn to her old habits.

RELATIONSHIP TO GOD

Another thing that helped her through this difficult transition was her growing faith in God. Blige had always believed in God, but now she was learning to believe something more: that God loved her and wanted the best for her. She didn't have to be perfect. She didn't have to be rich or successful.

She had often thought of herself as ugly, but now she believed that God didn't care what she looked like. He cared about how she acted. With that realization, she started to like herself. She saw beauty where she had once seen ugliness. In 2003, Blige told Yahoo! Music, "I'm going to say this: I'm not perfect. [But] I don't care what people say about me; I just want to be down with God."

Her father left the family when she was young, and she rarely saw him when she was growing up. But it didn't matter anymore. God, she said, became her real father. And although she turned her life around once she met Isaacs, she says it was God working through Isaacs.

Blige says God wants good things for her. In a 2006 interview with *Blender* magazine, she said, "My God is a God who wants me to have things. He wants me to bling! He wants me to be the hottest thing on the block . . . My God's the bomb!"

NO MORE DRAMA

Professionally, Blige was in the spotlight again with her fifth album, *No More Drama*. There was a little irony here. The title song sampled the theme song from *The Young and the Restless*, a popular television daytime drama. However, the album's

WE ARE ONE

Mary J. Blige was nominated for two awards at the 2002 Grammys. The song "Family Affair" got her a nod for Best R & B Vocal Performance, Female. She was also up for Best R & B Album, with *No More Drama*. She didn't win in either category, but she still made an impression at the awards ceremony. Her live performance of the title song from *No More Drama* stunned the audience.

She belted out the song's powerful lyrics. It was almost like she forgot she was singing a song. "I walked out on stage, and I don't know what happened after that," she told *Entertainment Weekly* magazine in 2003. "It may have looked like I was there, but I wasn't . . . . I can't really watch [the tape]. I'm just like, 'Whoa! That ain't me.' I guess I used that moment to say, 'We are one.'"

If the vocals suffered a little bit during the performance, the audience didn't care. There was no way that they could miss the raw honesty that Blige was putting forth. She got a standing ovation. She had booted the drama out of her personal life. But with her music, she brought all that drama onstage.

Blige's raw, emotional performance of her hit song "No More Drama" was the talk of the 2002 Grammy Awards.

overall message was about getting rid of negative drama and focusing on the positive.

Another song on the album was a milestone for her. The danceable "Family Affair" gave Blige her very first number-one single on the Billboard Top 100. There was one thing about this song that she later regretted: one of the lyrics talked about getting drunk.

Critics liked the album, but it didn't sell as well as the record company had hoped. After a few months, the company repackaged it and gave it a new release. This time, it sold well and Blige was right back in a familiar place: the world of double-platinum albums.

Personally, she was in an unfamiliar place, but it was a good one. Her life was calm. In a time when celebrities meet, date, and marry within a few months, she and Isaacs took their time. They married on December 7, 2003, more than three years after they met. With the marriage, Blige gained three stepchildren: Nas, Jordan, and Briana. She has also said that she might like to have more children with Isaacs.

In 2002, Blige was at home—singing, of course. But she heard something different from the usual. The sound coming from her was something that she hadn't heard in years. She heard the voice she'd had as a child. Years of hard living had buried it, but now it had come back. She found herself reaching higher and higher notes. As she grew as a person, she grew as a singer.

She had come out on top. The proof was in her voice.

CHAPTER FOUR
KEEPING IT REAL

Mary J. Blige had gone from being a star to being a superstar. Fellow musician Sting called her the "heir to Aretha [Franklin]." Other musicians asked her to contribute to their work. She sang on albums for Will Smith, Missy Elliott, LL Cool J, Ludacris, and her longtime friend Sean "Diddy" Combs. She and Elton John revisited his classic, "I Guess That's Why They Call It the Blues." She also teamed up with Sting on "Whenever I Say Your Name," and with Aretha Franklin on "Never Gonna Break My Faith."

Her career was steaming along, but more important, she was happy in her life. As always with Blige, her next album title, *Love & Life*, said so.

BREAKING THROUGH

She didn't always get along with Combs, her very first producer, but he was like family. They would fight, and then they would forgive. And with music, Blige recognized that she and Combs had a certain "chemistry." They reunited on *Love & Life*, her

Blige, pictured here with soul legend Aretha Franklin, has earned the respect of fellow musicians.

sixth album. It was released in 2003. Her record company had high hopes for the album. When she was promoting it, she told *Rolling Stone*, "Expect to be uplifted."

But music critics weren't impressed with *Love & Life*. Neither were her fans. The album did not sell well. Later, Blige said that she was pushed into making the wrong decisions. "I don't believe I was being as honest with my fans as I normally am," she told MTV in 2005, two years after the album came out. "That little feeling you get inside of you saying, 'Don't do it' — I didn't listen to it."

Although she split professionally from her first producer, Sean Combs *(above, left)*, Blige recognized a musical "chemistry" that brought them together again for 2003's *Love & Life*.

Some said that the new, happy Mary J. Blige wasn't good for her music. Pain was the subject of so many of her moving songs. But pain no longer ruled her life. Did she have nothing left to say? Blige refused to apologize for being happy. Instead, her answer came in the form of her seventh studio album, *The Breakthrough*, which came out in December 2005.

Despite the disappointment of *Love & Life*, Blige decided to work with Combs again on this album. The decision paid off. *The Breakthrough* was her biggest album yet. And, as always, she was keeping it real.

The songs on *The Breakthrough* were both positive and honest. With this album, she showed the music world that pain was still a part of her—but now it was a part of her past. She was "breaking through"—on both a personal level and a musical one. She told VH1 in 2006, "Through it all, I've come to a place where I know that I'm gonna be alright."

The Breakthrough debuted at number one. It sold 727,000 copies in its first week. A single off the record, "Be Without You," stayed at number one on the R & B charts for longer than any song since 1949!

Blige was rewarded with eight Grammy Award nominations. At the 2007 ceremony, she took home the top prize in three categories: Best Vocal Performance, Best R & B Song, and Best R & B Album. She was in tears as she took the stage. "For so many years, I've been talked about negatively," she said. "But this time, I've been talked about positively."

A special addition to the album was Blige's duet with U2 frontman Bono, on U2's hit song "One." She acknowledged that the song wasn't her usual style of music, but she loved it and wanted to include it on the album. It was all part of the breakthrough.

AN INFLUENCE FOR A NEW GENERATION

In June 2007, Blige received another honor. ASCAP (American Society of Composers, Authors and Publishers) gave her its Voice of Music Award. For years, she had sung about the hard times of women, especially African American women. She had

WHAT'S ON MARY'S CD PLAYER?

Mary J. Blige grew up listening to soul and hip-hop, and she made a name for herself combining the sounds of both music genres. But like most great musicians, her listening tastes are a lot wider than what she sings.

Sure, there are her standbys: Aretha Franklin and Anita Baker, Stevie Wonder and Sam Cooke, Otis Redding and the Ohio Players. There's Earth, Wind & Fire and Kool & the Gang. "They give me fuel. Those people keep me going," she told VH1 in 2006. But there's also Elton John and the Eagles, and more modern rock from Coldplay and Maroon 5. She's very impressed with fellow soul singer Jill Scott.

Blige doesn't have trouble finding something to suit her mood or anyone else's. "I just throw in whatever I throw in and listen to it," she said in a 2003 interview with VH1. "Wherever you want to go. You think about it and I have it."

been in the trenches with them, and, if only for the length of a three-minute song, she had pulled them out. The ASCAP award, given to artists "whose music illuminates people's lives through song," was a fitting tribute to her work.

Many people talk about how artists have a social responsibility. Blige doesn't think artists automatically have to accept that

Blige accepts an award from ASCAP in 2007. Both fans and music professionals recognize her ability to touch her audience emotionally.

responsibility, but she wants to for herself. Her fans have listened to her and believed in her. They have taken her songs and used them to help them through difficult situations and to become better people. "I've got a responsibility to not hurt them," she told *Rolling Stone* in 2007.

Blige is also active with charity work. In 2000, she received *Rolling Stone*'s Do Something Award for her charity efforts, including helping to raise money for AIDS victims. In 2004, she recorded the Eric Clapton song "Tears in Heaven" as a way to raise money for the tsunami victims in Southeast Asia. The year 2005 found her helping in the relief efforts for Hurricane Katrina, which struck the United States. She's also helped out in the "Rap the Vote" campaign, which enlists musicians to reach out to young people to get them to vote in political elections.

Music isn't the only way that Blige touches an audience. For someone who has asked for "no more drama," she could be a member of the drama club with her several acting credits. In a 1998 appearance on *The Jamie Foxx Show*, she played a preacher's daughter who wanted to stretch beyond singing gospel music. Later, she starred in an independent movie, *Prison Song*, playing a rap artist, and then appeared on a Lifetime network show, *Strong Medicine*, about a sick singer who won't get help. In 2005, she was approached to star in an MTV movie about Nina Simone, a legendary African American singer who died in 2003.

Beyoncé, Alicia Keys, Lauryn Hill, Keyshia Cole, Ashanti, Faith Evans, and many other artists owe a debt to Blige. Knowing that she has a tremendous influence, Blige emphasizes that it's important to find your own way. "I listened to Chaka Khan and I listened to Aretha, but I don't sound like them," she told VH1 in 2001. "There's a difference. You gotta take what you need, love them and respect them, and build your own foundation with it. That's the message I want to give to every up-and-coming artist . . . When it's time, are you going to know how to give you?"

THE JOURNEY CONTINUES

When does a singer reach diva status? It's hard to pick an exact moment, but clearly Blige is up on the platform. She's been on VH1's *Divas Live* show, singing with divas including Whitney Houston, Tina Turner, and Cher. She sang with her childhood idol and fellow diva, Aretha Franklin, when the two appeared on the TV show of yet another diva, Oprah Winfrey.

In 2007, her friend Jada Pinkett-Smith threw a party for her, inviting Winfrey and other famous guests. The party had a name: "The Celebrate Mary J. Blige Party."

Blige may be a diva, but she's trying not to act like one. A few years ago, a friend suggested that Winfrey interview her for *O*, her monthly magazine. But Winfrey said no. She sensed that Blige wasn't ready. In 2006, when Winfrey finally did the interview, Blige was ready to be honest about herself and with herself. Winfrey said, "I know transformation when I see it. Clearly, she's Mary J., rising. A woman ascending to full possession of herself."

In 2007, she put out her eighth album, *Growing Pains*. Life is full of them, and Blige can be counted on to tell her fans all about its ups and downs. How are things now? As always with Mary J., just take a look at her song titles: the hit single "Just Fine" gives the answer.

She's at a good place in her life journey. She and Isaacs now live in Hollywood Hills, California. She loves to relax in the

Years after their marriage, Mary J. Blige and Kendu Isaacs still work together on her music.

peaceful environment, but she's also found that it's a great place to work. Sometimes, the journey is just a short walk down the hallway. For the song "We Ride," she and Isaacs used the studio that they have in their house. She sang the song while wearing her nightgown. After years of heartache and hard work, Blige has earned those kinds of simple rewards. She's built a successful career, found a loving husband, and created the peace she wanted.

Yes, she's doing just fine.

TIMELINE

1971 Mary J. Blige is born in the Bronx, New York.

1989 She signs with Uptown Records.

1990s Hip-hop soul emerges as a subgenre of R & B.

1992 She releases her debut album, *What's the 411?*.

1993 She is named Best New Artist at the Soul Train Music Awards.

1994 Blige teams up with Sean "Diddy" Combs to produce *My Life*.

1996 She wins her first Grammy Award for the duet with Method Man, "I'll Be There for You/You're All I Need to Get By."

1997 She breaks from Combs to go solo on her third album, *Share My World*.

2000 *Rolling Stone* gives Blige its Do Something Award to recognize her charity work; she meets Kendu Isaacs.

2001 She gives up drugs and alcohol; "Family Affair" becomes her first number one single on the pop charts; she stars with hip-hop artist Q-Tip in the independent movie *Prison Song*.

2002 She gives an emotional performance of "No More Drama" at the Grammy Awards and receives a standing ovation.

2003 She marries Isaacs; she reunites with Combs to produce *Love & Life*.

2005 On *The Breakthrough*, Blige sings with U2's frontman Bono on the song "One."

2007 Blige is nominated for eight Grammy Awards and wins three, including Best R & B Album and Best R & B Song; she wins the Voice of Music Award from ASCAP.

DISCOGRAPHY

1992	*What's the 411?* (Uptown/MCA)
1994	*My Life* (Uptown/MCA)
1997	*Share My World* (MCA)
1999	*Mary* (MCA)
2001	*No More Drama* (MCA)
2003	*Love & Life* (Geffen)
2005	*The Breakthrough* (Geffen)
2007	*Growing Pains* (Geffen)

GLOSSARY

bling Flashy, expensive clothing and accessories that create an image of wealth and success.

break The part of a song in between the lyrics, usually with a strong beat.

crossover Successful in more than one genre.

diva An influential female superstar.

etiquette Proper manners.

genre A category.

gold A record that has sold five hundred thousand copies.

harmonize Singing or playing notes that blend with the melody.

hip-hop An urban cultural movement that includes rap music, break dancing, and street art.

hook A line repeated throughout a song.

illuminate To shed light on; draw attention to.

legendary Describes something or someone famous because of historical importance.

mixer A sound device used to blend two pieces of music.

nominate To suggest for an award.

platinum A term for a record that has sold one million copies.

repertoire A list or collection.

sampling Using part of a song in another song.

scratching Moving a record underneath the needle to create a scratchy noise.

soul An emotional kind of music that originated with African Americans.

turntable A record player.

FOR MORE INFORMATION

Hip-Hop Association
P.O. Box 1181
New York, NY 10035
(212) 500-5970
E-mail: info@hiphopassociation.org
Web site: http://www.hiphopassociation.org
The Harlem, New York–based Hip-Hop Association uses hip-hop
    culture to empower communities and forward change.

Web Sites

Due to the changing nature of Internet links, Rosen Publishing
has developed an online list of Web sites related to the subject
of this book. This site is updated regularly. Please use this link to
access this list:

http://www.rosenlinks.com/lhhb/maryj

FOR FURTHER READING

Baker, Soren. *The History of Rap and Hip-Hop*. Farmington Hills, MI: Lucent, 2006.

Brown, Terrell. *Mary J. Blige*. Broomall, PA: Mason Crest Publishers, 2007.

Payment, Simone. *Queen Latifah*. New York, NY: Rosen Publishing, 2006.

Torres, Jennifer. *Mary J. Blige*. Hockessin, DE: Mitchell Lane Publishers, 2008.

Vibe Books. *Hip-Hop Divas*. New York, NY: Three Rivers Press, 2001.

Waters, Rosa. *Hip-Hop: A Short History*. Broomall, PA: Mason Crest Publishers, 2007.

Wolny, Philip. *Sean Combs*. New York, NY: Rosen Publishing, 2006.

BIBLIOGRAPHY

Amber, Jeannine. "Mary Full of Grace." *Essence*, September 2005, pp. 172–176.

Chappell, Kevin. "Mary J. Blige: A New Man, a New Career—and No More Drama." *Ebony*, August 2002. Retrieved November 20, 2007 (http://findarticles.com/p/articles/mi_m1077/is_10_57/ai_97997627).

Chappell, Kevin. "Mary J. Blige's Tearful Plea: I've Got to Be Me." *Ebony*, October 2003.

Edwards, Gavin. "The Continuing Drama of Mary J. Blige." RollingStone.com, March 10, 2006. Retrieved November 20, 2007 (http://www.rollingstone.com/news/story/9447919/the_continuing_drama_of_mary_j_blige).

Eliscu, Jenny. "Mary J. Blige Rules." RollingStone.com, August 13, 2003. Retrieved November 20, 2007 (http://www.rollingstone.com/artists/maryjblige/articles/story/5935352/mary_j_blige_rules).

Ford, Tracey. "Mary J. Blige Hits Career High." RollingStone.com, January 3, 2006. Retrieved November 20, 2007 (http://www.rollingstone.com/artists/maryjblige/articles/story/9100416/mary_j_blige_hits_career_high).

Gregory, Deborah. "Proud Mary." *Essence*, March 1995, pp. 64–66, 124.

Johnson, Billy Jr. "Mary Speaks About Love & Life." Yahoo! Music, August 17, 2003. Retrieved November 15, 2007 (http://music.yahoo.com/read/interview/12028274).

Lelinwalla, Mark. "Mary J. Blige: All Hail the Queen." BallerStatus.com, January 3, 2006. Retrieved December 13, 2007 (http://www. ballerstatus.com/article/features/2006/01/2132/).

Macnie, Jim, and C. Bottomley. "Mary J. Blige: The Greatest Love of All." VH1.com, July 14, 2003. Retrieved November 15, 2007 (http://www. vh1.com/artists/interview/1473710/07102003/blige_mary_j.jhtml).

Mayo, Kierna. "Real Love: Mary J. Blige and Kendu Isaacs." *Essence*, June 2007, pp. 136–145.

Parade.com. "You Can Find a Way to Heal." February 4, 2007. Retrieved November 20, 2007. (http://www.parade.com/articles/editions/ 2007/edition_02-04-2007/Mary_J._Blige).

Powers, Ann. "Dear Superstar: Mary J. Blige." Blender.com, May 2006. Retrieved December 13, 2007 (http://www.blender.com/guide/ articles.aspx?id=1910).

RockOnTheNet.com. "Mary J. Blige." Retrieved November 15, 2007 (http://www.rockonthenet.com/artists-b/maryjblige_main.htm).

Udovitch, Mim. "God, PMS & Mary J. Blige." RollingStone.com, November 7, 2001. Retrieved November 20, 2007 (http://www.rollingstone.com/ artists/maryjblige/articles/story/5920021/god_pms__mary_j_blige).

Williams, Zoe. "Quite Contrary." *Guardian* (UK), December 17, 2005. Retrieved November 20, 2007 (http://arts.guardian.co.uk/features/ story/0,,1669258,00.html).

Winfrey, Oprah. "The O Interview: Oprah Talks to Mary J. Blige." O, May 2006, pp. 240–243, 304, 306.

INDEX

ABOUT THE AUTHOR

Like Mary J., Diane Bailey was a child when hip-hop sprang onto the music scene. She still listens to "Rapper's Delight" every once in a while, and she still plays her music too loud. Bailey has two children and writes on a variety of nonfiction topics.

PHOTO CREDITS

Cover Jeff Kravitz/FilmMagic; p. 1 Gabriel Bouys/AFP/Getty Images; p. 7 Ian Tyas/Keystone/Hulton Archive/Getty Images; p. 9 Leo Vals/ Hulton Archive/Getty Images; pp. 13, 15 Chi Modu/diverseimages/ Getty Images; pp.19, 35 © AP Images; p. 21 Stefan Zaklin/Getty Images; p. 23 Peter Kramer/Getty Images; p. 25 Frederick M. Brown/ Getty Images; pp. 28, 32 Kevin Winter/Getty Images; p. 31 Frank Micelotta/Getty Images; p. 38 Stephen Shugerman/Getty Images.

Designer: Tom Forget; Editor: Bethany Bryan
Photo Researcher: Cindy Reiman